Fishy Wishes

YOUNG YEARLING BOOKS YOU WILL ENJOY:

The Pee Wee Scout Books by Judy Delton

YEARLING BOOKS/YOUNG YEARLINGS/YEARLING CLASSICS are designed especially to entertain and enlighten young people. Patricia Reilly Giff, consultant to this series, received her bachelor's degree from Marymount College and a master's degree in history from St. John's University. She holds a Professional Diploma in Reading and a Doctorate of Humane Letters from Hofstra University. She was a teacher and reading consultant for many years, and is the author of numerous books for young readers.

For a complete listing of all Yearling titles, write to Dell Readers Service, P.O. Box 1045, South Holland, IL 60473.

Fishy Wishes

JUDY DELTON

Illustrated by Alan Tiegreen

A YOUNG YEARLING BOOK

Published by
Dell Publishing
a division of
Bantam Doubleday Dell Publishing Group, Inc.
1540 Broadway
New York, New York 10036

The trademark Yearling® is registered in the U.S. Patent and Trademark Office.
The trademark Dell® is registered in the U.S. Patent and Trademark Office.

ISBN: 0-440-40850-4

Printed in the United States of America

September 1993

10 9 8 7 6 5 4 3 2

CWO

For Elm, the card sunfish, from the shark

Contents

Fishy Wishes

CHAPTER 1

The New Pee Wee

"Hey, who's that kid with the wheels?" shouted Roger White. "What's he doing here?"

Mrs. Peters frowned at Roger, as she always did when someone said something he or she shouldn't have said.

It was Tuesday, and Tuesday was the meeting day of the Pee Wee Scouts. They met in Mrs. Peters's basement after school. Mrs. Peters was the leader of Troop 23.

"Maybe he's a visitor," said Molly Duff to her best friend, Mary Beth Kelly.

The girls looked at the boy sitting in the wheelchair at the big table.

"We don't need any more kids in our troop," said Tim Noon. "There won't be enough cupcakes."

The rest of the Pee Wees clambered down the steps and sat down in their chairs. They all looked surprised to see the wheelchair.

Scrape, bump, scrape went the chairs on the floor. Roger tipped way back in his, and Mrs. Peters frowned at him again. Once Roger had tipped right over and landed on his head on the floor.

Mrs. Peters clapped her hands.

"Boys and girls, I have some news for you today. We have a new Scout with us for the next few months. His name is Jody George. I hope that you will all make him feel welcome in Troop 23."

First no one said anything. Then Roger put his fingers in his mouth and whistled a long, piercing, shrieking whistle. The rest of the Pee Wees clapped.

"What kind of a name is that?" asked Sonny Betz Stone. "Is George his last name or his middle name?"

"Hey, look who's talking about names, Stone," said Roger. "Sonny Rock, Sonny Pebble, Sonny Boulder."

"How can this guy play ball against Troop 15?" asked Tim.

"Jody's a girl's name," said Tracy Barnes. "I never heard of a boy named Jody."

All of a sudden Rachel Meyers got up from her chair and walked up to Jody. Her curls bounced as she walked.

"Welcome to Pee Wee Scouts," she said. "We are glad to have you here."

Rat's knees! thought Molly. Why didn't I think of doing that? But Molly knew that even if she had, she wouldn't have had the nerve to go up and say it. Rachel had lots of self-confidence and a lot of nerve. Molly was shy.

Now Rachel was writing her name and address and phone number on a piece of her ballerina stationery. She handed it to Jody.

"Call me anytime," she said. Then she walked back to her chair.

Now Tracy was going up to Jody. "Glad you're here," she said.

Tim went up and gave him a broken pencil.

"Some gift," whispered Mary Beth.

Kevin Moe went up to Jody. Molly liked Kevin. She wanted to marry him when she grew up. Kevin was smart. He was going to be mayor someday.

"Glad to have you aboard," said Kevin.

Mary Beth giggled.

"We're Scouts, not sailors," she said.

"That's political," whispered Molly. "Kevin is a politician."

She didn't like Mary Beth giggling at Kevin.

Now Lisa Ronning was shaking Jody's hand. And the Baker twins, Kenny and Patty. Pretty soon everyone had welcomed Jody but Roger and Molly.

Roger swaggered up and said, "What kind of a name is that? Is George your last name or your middle name?"

"My last name," said Jody.

"How can you play ball in a wheelchair?" Kenny was asking.

"I can go pretty fast," he replied.

5

"My cousin's in a wheelchair," said Rachel. "It's an electric one. She can go anywhere she wants."

"So can I," said Jody. "I go on boats and airplanes all the time."

Molly was getting nervous. Even Mary Beth had gone up to meet Jody. Finally she got all her courage together and went up to his wheelchair.

"Do you sleep in there too?" was the only thing that came to her to say.

"Ho, ho, ho." Roger laughed. "Sure, Duff, he sleeps sitting up."

Now Roger sat up straight in his chair and began to snore. Soon all the Pee Wees were snorting and snoring.

"I do sleep in it sometimes," said Jody. "The back goes down like this." He pushed a button, and the chair looked like Molly's dad's recliner.

Roger looked sheepish. Molly felt better. She hated to be laughed at.

"Now," said Mrs. Peters. "We will all get

6

into a circle and sing our Pee Wee Scout song."

The Pee Wees joined hands to sing. Kevin ran to take Jody's hand. Lisa and Tracy fought over his other hand.

Rachel ran up to the piano and took the sheet with words to the song from the top and gave it to Jody.

"Leader's pet," said Tim.

" 'Scouts are helpers, Scouts have fun,' " sang the Scouts to the tune of "Old MacDonald."

". . . Pee Wee, Pee Wee Scouts!
We sing and play when work is done,
Pee Wee, Pee Wee Scouts!

"With a good deed here,
And an errand there,
Here a hand, there a hand,
Everywhere a good hand.

"Scouts are helpers, Scouts have fun,
Pee Wee, Pee Wee Scouts!"

"Now for our pledge," said Mrs. Peters.

Roger ran and got the words for the pledge and handed them to Jody.

"We love our country
And our home,
Our school and neighbors too.

"As Pee Wee Scouts
We pledge our best
In everything we do."

When they had finished, Molly said, "Rat's knees! First no one wanted to be Jody's friend. Now everyone wants to. Roger is doing that for attention."

"I suppose," said Mary Beth. "But if a Scout isn't a friend to a new kid, who is?"

Molly was embarrassed for the second time that day. Mary Beth was right. It was up to Scouts to be helping and friendly. If anyone could do it, the Pee Wees could.

CHAPTER **2**

Mrs. Peters's News

Molly didn't know that people in wheelchairs could sing. But Jody seemed to sing as loud as the rest of the Pee Wees. She wondered what else he could do that she didn't know about.

Mrs. Peters clapped her hands.

"Boys and girls," she said. "It's time to tell the good deeds we've done all week. Who would like to be first?"

Hands waved. Before she could call on anyone, Rachel said, "Mrs. Peters, I raked our yard and our neighbor's yard. Our neighbor didn't even ask me to—I just did it."

"Hey, dummy, how did you know he

11

wanted his yard raked?" said Roger. "Maybe he wanted flat grass!"

Rachel stuck out her tongue at Roger. Mrs. Peters frowned.

"Who wants all kinds of garbage and junk all over their lawn?" said Rachel. "Probably *you* would."

Mrs. Peters called on Tim before there was any more arguing.

"I raked my grass," said Tim.

"Copycat!" said Rachel. "You did not! You just said that because I said that."

"Did too!" said Tim.

"Did not!" said Rachel.

Mrs. Peters sighed and held up her hand.

"Tim could have raked his yard too," she said. "Let's move on."

"I washed my dad's car," said Patty Baker.

"And I vacuumed the inside of it," said Kenny.

"Very nice!" said Mrs. Peters. "That is surely a very good deed."

Rat's knees. Molly wished she could have done that. But her dad had had the car washed at the Nice an' Easy car wash. Some workers with rags and brooms had cleaned it inside and out while it moved down a long track. It cost money. Molly could have done it for nothing.

"I gave the twins some of my candy," said Sonny. "I shared," he added, in case that did not seem generous enough.

"Your twins are too little to eat candy," said Kevin. "They could have choked, Stone. You could have killed them!"

Sonny didn't look as if he liked having his good deed turned into attempted murder.

Roger started coughing and choking and holding his throat. Then he fell over and pretended he was dead. Soon all the Pee Wees were choking and coughing and falling over dead.

Sonny looked as if he might cry. "It was soft candy," he said. "It melts in your mouth. Anyway, I didn't kill them."

"What a baby," said Mary Beth. "Sonny can't take a joke at all."

"It's not a joke to be accused of murder," said Molly. "I wouldn't like that either."

Molly usually defended Sonny. It wasn't his fault he was sensitive to jokes about being a baby.

"Well, let's just remember what we learned in our safety class," said Mrs. Peters. "When we are around small children, we must be careful of what they put in their mouths."

"I shoveled snow off the sidewalk," said Tracy.

The whole troop stared at her.

"It's summer," said Roger. "What kind of snow did you shovel, Barnes? Ivory Snow?" He laughed at his joke.

"It isn't summer, it's fall," said Rachel, who didn't want Roger to get away with anything. "It's September, and that's not summer."

"It was last winter when I shoveled it," said Tracy.

Molly wondered why she had waited till now to tell about it. But Mrs. Peters said, "Shoveling snow is a good, good deed."

Lisa said she had given her little cousin a bath.

Roger said he had built an addition onto his garage. No one believed him.

Molly told about dusting the bookshelves. "I took all the books off to do it," she said. "I didn't just dust around them. It was a lot of work to take them all off. And then I dusted the books too."

Mrs. Peters nodded seriously. But she didn't say it was a wonderful good deed.

Then Jody raised his hand. Everyone was as quiet as a pin. What good deed could someone in a wheelchair do?

"I read the comic strips to my little brother," he said.

So people in wheelchairs could read!

And they could have little brothers!

And they could do good deeds and have them to report, even though Jody hadn't known he would have to report a good deed!

Molly wasn't the only one who was shocked.

"Is your little brother in a wheelchair too?" asked Patty politely.

Suddenly Molly pictured an entire wheelchair family. Wheelchairs around the breakfast table.

Wheelchairs doing the dishes.

Wheelchairs lined up in a row for a family picture.

Wheelchairs around a Christmas tree . . .

"No," said Jody. "I'm the only handicapped person in my family."

Molly's imagination had run away with her again. Her mother called her imagination "wild."

"Now," said Mrs. Peters, "it's time for refreshments."

The Pee Wees immediately forgot good deeds and yelled "Yeah!" at the top of their lungs.

Sonny's mother came down the basement steps, carrying a big plate of cupcakes with autumn leaves on them made of frosting. Mrs. Stone was the assistant troop leader. She set them on the table and tied a napkin around

Sonny's neck that looked like a bib. The Pee Wees dug in. Mrs. Peters poured glasses of milk to go with the treat.

"Now, while you are enjoying your treat," said their leader, "I'm going to give you some news. You must be wondering what badge we are going to earn next!"

All the Pee Wees nodded, with cupcake in their mouths. They loved to earn badges.

"How many of you have hobbies?" she asked.

A few hands waved. Rachel's waved wildly.

"Mrs. Peters, I have *four* hobbies," she said.

Of course, thought Molly. If someone had one hobby, Rachel had to have four.

Rachel rattled off all four: "Tap-dancing, skiing, skating, and reading."

"I read, but I never thought it was a *hobby*," said Tracy. "It's something we have to do in school. It's work."

"I hate to read," said Sonny.

"Ha, that's because you're such a baby you can only read 'Run, Spot, Run'!" said Roger.

Sonny was about to throw his cupcake at Roger when Mrs. Peters held up her hand.

Molly loved to read. She got piles of books from the library.

"Reading can be a hobby," said Mrs. Peters. "A hobby is something we do for pleasure, outside of our regular work. I've brought some pictures of many different hobbies."

While Mrs. Peters held up the pictures, Molly wondered what hobbies had to do with badges.

"You see, here is a little girl who raises goldfish," said their leader. "And here is a boy making model airplanes. And a girl making model cars."

Mrs. Peters held up pictures of children painting pictures and modeling with clay and swimming and hiking in the woods and doing magic tricks.

"I would like you to begin thinking about hobbies," she went on, "and find one you like. When you find a hobby you like and get it under way, you can tell us all about it and show it to us, and when you do it well, you will get a hobby badge."

Rachel stood up and waved her hand again.

"How can I ski in here?" she said. "How can I show you my skiing hobby?"

"Like this," said Roger, getting up and making swooshing noises around the room.

"You can tell us about it," said Mrs. Peters, guiding Roger back to his seat.

Rachel sat down in a pout.

"You have to see it," she said.

"Now, take your time finding the right hobby," said Mrs. Peters. "Go to the library and look through books. Ask your family and friends what hobbies they have."

"My mother plays golf," said Lisa. "I don't think she'd let me do that."

"My dad hunts," said Roger.

"That's disgusting!" said Lisa. "Hurting those little animals."

The Pee Wees booed Roger. He looked sorry he ever said his dad's hobby.

"Now for my other news," said Mrs. Peters. "Grandparents Day is coming up, and I thought as a special treat we'd have a little program for your grandparents. Each of you could make up a little poem or verse to recite, or draw a picture. If you are extra clever, you can combine what you do for Grandparents Day with your hobby!"

The Pee Wees all nodded as if they had just the right thing to do in mind. All but Molly. She didn't nod. She didn't have a hobby. And how could she combine Grandparents Day with a hobby she didn't have?

CHAPTER 3

Looking for a Hobby

"Well, I don't have any work to do for my hobby," said Rachel on the way home. "And I can just do one of my old tap-dances at the program, and my grandma will love it. She loves the way I dance."

"My grandpa and grandma can't come!" cried Mary Beth. "They live in Florida. How can I do a hobby at the program with no one to watch?"

Mary Beth looked as if she might burst into tears anytime.

"I'll share my grandma and grandpa with you," said Molly, putting her arm around her friend.

"It's not the same," said Mary Beth, shaking her head. "We're supposed to have our own grandparents. *Your* grandparents come to see *you.*"

"They can see you too, silly," said Roger. "You think they have tunnel vision, like they can only look at one person on a stage?"

Roger made a telescope with his hands and looked at Mary Beth up close to her face. She shoved him away.

"Unless they are really very very old," said Roger. "Then they won't see anyone at all on the stage, even Molly!"

"Roger White, my grandparents are not very very old!" said Molly, stamping her foot. She gave Roger a kick in the shin. "They hike and travel and take karate classes, and they see perfectly well! My grandpa hasn't even got glasses!"

"All right, already!" shouted Roger, grabbing his leg. "They can see, they can see!"

What was bothering Molly was not her grandparents' eyesight. It was Mrs. Peters's words: " *'If you are extra clever*, you can com-

bine what you do for Grandparents Day with your hobby.' "

Extra clever. Molly *was* extra clever. She was not going to be the only one who couldn't combine. Why, every day someone told her how clever and smart she was! Her mother, her father, her grandma, her teacher. She *had* to combine her hobby with the program.

And before she did that, she was going to have to find a hobby.

The next afternoon after school, she and Mary Beth went to the public library. Mary Beth was still moping about her missing grandparents.

They got lots of books out and put them on the table. They paged through all of them.

Mary Beth pointed to a picture of a boy pasting stamps into a stamp album.

Molly shook her head. Old canceled stamps didn't interest her. She used a stamp when she wrote a letter, but she didn't *love* stamps. One per letter was enough. Who wanted a whole book of them? *Bor*-ing.

She came to a picture of a girl making little dots on paper. "Learn a code" it said underneath. Dots and dashes did not seem like a good way to send messages. Why figure it all out when she could call them on the phone? Or send a letter? Or even a fax or an overnight express? S.O.S. was not for her.

Molly slammed the book shut.

"There are no hobbies in here I want," she whispered to Mary Beth.

"You're too fussy," said Mary Beth. "You don't need a *perfect* hobby."

Molly thought about that. If someone was *extra clever*, they would have a perfect hobby. Anyway, who would want a hobby that was no fun if hobbies were meant to be fun?

"But I *want* a perfect hobby," said Molly. "I'm not going to do something dumb like collect stamps."

"Suit yourself," said Mary Beth. "I'm going to make a vase out of a bleach bottle. Then I can send it to my grandparents, even if they aren't here."

Molly looked at her in shock. "A bleach

bottle?" she echoed. "An ugly plastic bleach-bottle vase?"

"Well, you paint it," said Mary Beth. "You paint fancy designs on it, and no one knows it was a bleach bottle."

Molly was disgusted. She wouldn't want to give her grandma a bouquet of flowers in a bleach-bottle vase, painted or not.

The librarian looked at the girls and put her finger to her lips. "Shh," she said.

"Let's go," said Mary Beth. "I want to get home and start collecting stuff for my hobby."

At the corner of her block, Mary Beth said good-bye to Molly. Molly walked home past the variety shop. She looked in the window. There was a display of pencils and notebooks for school. There were book bags and flower bulbs and sewing kits and yarn. But right in the middle was a fishbowl. In the bowl were brightly colored goldfish swimming back and forth and sparkling in the sun.

On the shelf with the bowl were bird cages and pet food and rubber bones and seaweed.

There were colored pebbles and little castles. There was a book about setting up an aquarium and raising fish.

A RELAXING HOBBY it said on a sign.

Fish! Molly could get a mother and father fish and they would have babies and Molly could sell them! It could be her hobby, and she could make money at the same time! She could prove she was extra clever to Mrs. Peters, because she would give her grandparents two of the baby fish on Grandparents Day! Could this be the perfect hobby?

Molly ran home to shake her piggy bank. Adding up all the dimes and nickels and quarters, she had exactly five dollars!

"Can I spend some of my money on goldfish?" she asked her mother.

"If you take care of them," her mother replied. "Remember the last time you had pets." Molly did. But these new fish were not exactly *pets*. They were a business!

Her mother gave her an extra dollar to spend. Then Molly dashed back to the store and bought a fishbowl. She bought the book too, and some stones for the bottom and a piece of the green seaweed. With food it came to over five dollars. But the fish were only thirty-nine cents each.

"I want a boy fish and a girl fish so they can have babies," Molly told the clerk with the net.

"The females aren't as bright," said the clerk, scooping one out of the tank that had small brown spots on her sides.

Molly wondered if the clerk meant the girl fish weren't as smart as the boys, or if he meant the color.

"You see how bright the males are," said the clerk, catching a bright orange fish in the net.

It didn't seem fair, but if Molly wanted baby fish, she couldn't get two bright orange ones. Besides, she felt sorry for the spotted girl fish.

"Sometimes we give the females away free," said the clerk. "On Saturdays."

It sounded as if girls weren't very impor-

tant, Molly thought. But if it wasn't for them, there wouldn't *be* any babies!

Molly couldn't wait till Saturday to start her new hobby. No, she would start now. She'd have to pay full price and her whole six dollars would be gone, but she would soon be head over heels in money, selling her babies.

The clerk wrapped the bowl and put the fish in a plastic bag with water and tied a knot in it. He gave Molly a snail free.

"It will keep the bowl clean," he said.

Molly hurried home. She tried not to jiggle the fish.

When her mother opened the door, she held up her purchases.

"I have a perfect hobby," she said. "When my fish have babies, I can sell them!"

Her mother looked at Molly's things.

"You have to remember to feed them every day and keep their bowl clean," her mother warned.

"I'll do that," said Molly. "I'm going to spend all my free time with my fish."

Molly's dad helped her set up the fishbowl

on the bookcase in her room. She put the pebbles in and the seaweed. She set the fish food beside the bowl. Then her dad helped her put the fish in.

"Pretty," he said. "Those are nice guys."

"One's a girl," said Molly. "The spotted one."

Molly sat in front of her fish and watched them swim. Back and forth. Back and forth. She gave them a tiny bit of food and watched them fight for it.

Now all she had to do was sit back and wait for the babies to come. She had only one tiny worry: What if they didn't come in time for Grandparents Day?

CHAPTER 4

Molly's Bad Day

Every morning Molly fed her fish. And every evening she looked to see if there were babies. There never were. Grandparents Day was getting closer and closer, and there was no sign of a baby fish.

On Tuesday, Molly went to her Scout meeting. Everyone was gathered around Jody's wheelchair. Molly suddenly wished she had a wheelchair. Everyone made a fuss over kids in wheelchairs.

After they sang and told good deeds, Mrs. Peters asked how the hobbies were coming. Hands waved in the air.

"I made this vase," said Mary Beth when

Mrs. Peters called on her. She held it up. It had two fake flowers in it.

"Good for you!" said Mrs. Peters. "That is very creative."

She called on Rachel.

"I'm just doing my regular hobbies," she said, "which I've had for ages." She tap-danced across the room, doing a step she called Shuffle Off to Buffalo.

"My hobby is emptying the garbage," said Tim.

The Pee Wees broke into laughter. Even Jody laughed.

"That's a chore," said Kevin. "That's not a hobby."

"Hey, Noon, are you giving your grandma a bag of garbage at the program?" yelled Roger. "Happy Grandparents Day!"

Poor Tim. Roger picked on him as much as Sonny. But then, thought Molly, he picked on everyone.

"My hobby is eating," said Sonny. He had his eye on the cupcakes on the table. "And collecting old pop bottles. I turn them in and get money."

"What a fine ecology hobby," said Mrs. Peters. "Keeping our country free of litter."

"How can you do that for Grandparents Day?" asked Lisa.

"I can," said Sonny. "I can go over to their house and pick up bottles and stuff on their lawn. It would be a good deed *and* a hobby!"

No one could argue with that. Sonny did combine the hobby with Grandparents Day.

Roger had a piece of wood with him. He held it up.

"This is my hobby," he said.

The Pee Wees looked at the wood. It had little holes in it, all in a row.

"What is it?" asked Kenny.

"Those holes are cavities," said Roger. "I'm going to be a dentist, and my dad let me use his drill to practice." He passed the piece of wood around.

"Of course, when I get good, I'm going to drill on real teeth," he added.

"Not on mine, you're not, White!" shouted Kenny.

Roger was drilling into a piece of Styrofoam now with a pencil. "Bzzzzz," he said.

"Who would let Roger drill their teeth?" whispered Mary Beth.

"No one," Molly agreed.

Now Roger was pretending to drill into Mrs. Peters's table with a fork.

Jody told about collecting compact discs.

"I get them for my birthday and Christmas, and I buy them with money I earn at the garden center."

"Can you cut grass for people?" asked Patty politely.

Jody shook his head. "My aunt owns the store, and I pot plants and get boxes ready for the deliveries. Sometimes I fertilize the plants and spray them."

The Pee Wees looked surprised. Jody was the only Pee Wee with an honest-to-goodness job! For money!

"I go to concerts too, when my favorite

39

groups come to town," Jody went on. "And sometimes my parents take me to the city."

Jody had a pretty exciting life, thought Molly. More exciting than people who could walk! But Jody had even more to say: He told the Pee Wees about his compact disc parties at his house and how he played the guitar.

"Not real well," he said, "but I'm learning. Someday I'd like to play with a rock band."

After Jody's hobbies, the other Pee Wees' hobbies seemed tame.

Molly told about her fish, and Mrs. Peters didn't seem as excited as Molly thought she should be.

"It isn't easy to raise fish," said Tracy. "Unless they're guppies. Guppies have babies by the zillions."

"But guppies aren't as pretty as goldfish," said Molly.

"Yes, they are!" said Tracy.

"No, they're not," replied Molly.

Mrs. Peters clapped her hands. "Other hobbies?" she asked.

Some of the Pee Wees didn't have hobbies yet.

"I can't think of anything," said Patty.

"You can collect things," offered Mrs. Peters. "Like leaves or rocks or pictures of pets."

Lisa's hand was waving.

"Mrs. Peters?" she said. "My aunt collects salt and pepper shakers! She's got about a hundred pairs. She's got these little grapefruits from Florida and potatoes from Idaho and this little dog and cat, and one set is real sterling silver."

Who in the world would need a hundred pairs of salt and pepper shakers? thought Molly. At her house there was one set on the stove and one on the table, and that was enough salt for anyone's baked potato.

"How could you use all that salt and pepper?" asked Molly.

"They aren't to *use*," said Lisa. "They're to look at."

A hundred pairs salt and pepper shakers filled with salt and pepper just to look at? That seemed like a real waste to Molly. What

41

good was something if you didn't *use* it? Besides, you look at pictures and sunsets and lakes. You don't look at salt shakers.

But Mrs. Peters seemed to think it was a fine hobby and said that she used to collect salt and pepper shakers too!

"What a dumb hobby," Molly said to Mary Beth on the way home. "I hate salt and pepper shakers."

"Well, fish aren't so great either," said Mary Beth. "You don't like anything."

Molly felt hurt. She wanted to cry. Did she really hate everything? Was she going to fight with her best friend over some dumb salt and pepper shakers, of all things?

"My mother collects them too," Mary Beth went on, "and she collects little silver spoons from every state."

Molly wondered what she used all those spoons for. It must be like the shakers: nothing. Just to look at.

"Well, I don't *hate* them," said Molly.

"Yes, you do," said Mary Beth.

Now it was Mary Beth who was hurt. Be-

fore Molly could say anything else, her friend turned the corner and ran toward her own home without even saying good-bye.

"Rat's knees!" shouted Molly out loud to no one. "I have no baby fish, and my best friend is mad at me!"

Molly kicked the curb as she crossed the street. It wasn't a good day.

And when she got home, her orange goldfish was dead.

CHAPTER 5

Trying Again

At first Molly thought her fish was sleeping. But when she gave him food, he didn't eat it. He just lay on top of the water, and his bright orange didn't look bright anymore.

"My fish died!" called Molly to her mom and dad.

They came to look.

"And I took good care of him," Molly said, sobbing.

"It was nothing you did," said Mr. Duff. "Pets die. Maybe he was an old fish, or maybe he missed the other fish. It could have been anything."

Molly's dad scooped the fish out of the

45

bowl and took it away. Now the girl fish looked lonely. She swam around through the seaweed, looking for her friend.

"How can I have babies now?" said Molly.

Her mother and dad had no answer for that.

The next day Molly's dad came home from work with a plastic bag full of water, and in the water was a brand-new fish that looked something like the first one, except that the new one had black marks on his tail.

"This one looks healthier," said her dad. He emptied the bag into the bowl.

"He's pretty," admitted Molly. She gave her dad a hug. Maybe there was hope for babies yet.

"If at first you don't succeed . . ." said her father.

"Try, try again," said her mother.

Molly fed her fish every morning. And every evening she looked for babies. But instead of baby fish, there seemed to be baby snails. One, two, three, four snails. Before long there were thirty snails, and then Molly stopped counting. Pretty soon she could hardly see the fish because there were so many snails.

Mrs. Duff shook her head. So did Mr. Duff.

"Maybe you should sell snails instead of fish," he suggested.

But no one wanted to buy snails. They were not pretty, and they did not swim, as fish did. And surely her grandparents would not want snails for a present!

Now she had a new problem, and she couldn't even talk it over with her best friend, because her best friend wasn't talking to her. Molly's eyes filled with tears, and after her parents left, she tried to take the snails out of the bowl with the little fishnet. No matter how many she took out, there seemed to be just as many remaining.

As she was lying on her bed feeling sad, she saw her fish book on the bookshelf. She had forgotten all about it. She took it off the shelf and opened it.

Chapter one was about setting up the aquarium. Molly did not have an aquarium. She had a fishbowl. She did not have a char-

coal filter. She did not have a heater. Or a light. Or a thermometer.

"No wonder my fish died!" she said out loud.

She showed the book to her parents.

"It looks like we should have read this before we got the fish," said her dad.

"Raising fish is harder than we thought," said Mrs. Duff.

" 'Snails in the aquarium keep the sides of the aquarium clean,' " read her father. " 'But beware of too many snails. A catfish or algae eater can do the same job and not multiply as fast.' "

"What does it say to do if you already have too many snails?" asked Molly.

Her dad paged through the book.

"Snail killer," he said.

"I don't want to kill those baby snails!" said Molly.

"It says goldfish rarely breed in a fishbowl," said Mr. Duff.

"Maybe there's another hobby that you'd like better," said Molly's mother kindly.

How could her mother say that about her extra-clever hobby? The hobby it took her so long to find? The hobby she had spent all her money on?

"I don't want another hobby!" shouted Molly. "I want to raise fish!"

She ran to her room and threw herself onto her bed. In a little while her dad came in.

"You are taking this whole hobby thing too seriously," he said. "Hobbies are supposed to be fun. They don't have to be perfect."

So Mary Beth was right. She was being a baby about this.

"I'll try to find a new home for them if you want to try something else," he said.

Molly nodded.

Her father took the fishbowl and the fish book and the food away.

Molly knew what she had to do. She had to tell Mary Beth she was sorry she criticized her mother's hobby. And she had to find a new hobby for herself, even if it wasn't perfect. Even if she wasn't wild about it. She had to get that badge.

Molly dialed her friend's number.

"I'm sorry," she blurted out. "I'm sorry about the salt and pepper shakers."

The way Molly felt right now, she wouldn't mind having a collection of them for her own.

"It's okay," said Mary Beth. "But don't make fun of my bleach bottles again either."

"I won't," said Molly. "Can you help me find a new hobby? My fish wouldn't breed and I got piles of snails."

"You could knit," said Mary Beth. "The lady next door to us knits lots of these really pretty sweaters. She could show you how."

Molly had lots of sweaters in her drawer. But she didn't want to find fault with another hobby that Mary Beth suggested. That was what had gotten her in trouble to start with.

"Okay," said Molly. "My mom has some yarn in her sewing basket."

"Really?" said Mary Beth, glad to have Molly accept her suggestion. "I'll call Mrs. Beal and tell her."

All night Molly thought about the pretty sweaters she would knit. And then she had an extra-clever idea: She could knit sweaters for her grandma and grandpa! They would like that better than fish, and it would combine her hobby and Grandparents Day! Her grandma loved blue. She would make hers blue, and her grandpa's red! She couldn't wait to begin. If she made extra sweaters, she could sell them!

At Mrs. Beal's house the next day, Molly saw rows and rows of bright sweaters hanging in a row. Sweaters with reindeer on them. Sweaters with trees and cats and snowflakes.

"I'd like to do the reindeer," she said to Mrs. Beal.

Mrs. Beal laughed and said, "Someday, someday."

What did she mean, someday? Someday was *now*.

She'd brought yarn from her mother, and needles from Mary Beth's aunt, and now she sat and watched Mrs. Beal cast on.

"We'll start with just ten stitches," she said, smiling.

"Is that enough for a sweater?" asked Molly.

"Oh my, we can't begin with a *sweater*!" She laughed. "We have to begin with a straight little scarf. For a baby."

Molly did not want to make something for a baby. It wasn't Babies Day she needed to prepare for, it was Grandparents Day.

"We'll knit a row and purl a row, knit a row and purl a row," sang Mrs. Beal as Molly watched.

Pretty soon Molly could do it. But not as fast as Mrs. Beal. And not as neatly. Some of her stitches were too tight, and some were too loose. And some she lost altogether when they slid off the needles and disappeared.

"That's fine!" said Mrs. Beal. "It will even up as you go along. Knit a row, purl a row, knit a row, purl a row."

"I think I can do it alone now!" said Molly. She thanked Mrs. Beal and left to show Mary Beth what she'd learned.

"Practice, practice, practice," called Mrs. Beal. "Practice makes perfect, you know.

Come again tomorrow afternoon for lesson two."

But Molly didn't need two lessons. She already knew how to knit. She'd just keep knitting till she finished.

When she got to Mary Beth's house, she said, "She taught me how to knit a baby scarf. But I want a sweater."

"Well, that doesn't look like a baby scarf to me," said her friend. "It could be a sleeve of a sweater, couldn't it, if you made it longer and then sewed it up the side?"

Mary Beth was a genius! Molly was making a sweater, and she didn't even know it!

All afternoon Mary Beth painted pretty pictures on her vase.

All afternoon Molly sat beside her and knit a sleeve. Sometimes she forgot if she was knitting or purling. And sometimes she dropped a stitch. But one thing was for sure: The sleeve was getting longer! This was a wonderful hobby, and she owed it all to Mary Beth! She wanted to reach over and hug her.

All week Molly knit. Before school and after school. Before supper and after supper.

"How is your hobby coming?" asked her mother one evening.

"Fine," she said. She didn't want to show her mother yet. She wanted it to be a surprise. Think how proud her mother would be that Molly had a successful hobby! Think how surprised Mrs. Peters would be! And her grandma and grandpa! Molly got the shivers just thinking about it!

The day before the Pee Wee Scout meeting, Molly finished both sleeves. She sewed them up with a needle and thread. She would have to quickly knit the back of the sweater and the front. She wanted to show it at the meeting. She got knitting and purling mixed up, but she kept going.

She knit at night and in the morning and during recess at school. The back of the sweater was still very small. But she had to sew the sleeves onto it, or no one would know it was a sweater. She pulled it to make it bigger. Then she sewed the sleeves on quickly. She stuffed it into her book bag and joined the other Pee Wees on the way to Mrs. Peters's house.

CHAPTER 6

Wheelchair Whoopee

When they got there, Jody's father was carrying Jody down the steps into Mrs. Peters's basement. He set him on a regular chair at the table and went back to get the folded-up wheelchair.

He set the wheelchair up in the basement in case Jody needed it, and waved good-bye.

"Be good!" he called, smiling.

"Hey, look at me!" shouted Roger, sitting in Jody's wheelchair and pushing off from a wall with his arms. He went sailing around the basement.

Before anyone could stop them, the rest of the boys clamored for a turn.

"Wheeee!" shouted Sonny, going around in circles in the chair.

Mrs. Peters clapped her hands. She looked cross. Very cross.

"That is not your property, is it?" she said sternly. "And it is rude as well."

The boys stopped riding in the chair. Mrs. Peters stared at Roger until he apologized to Jody.

"It's all right," said Jody. "Lots of people like to ride in my wheelchair."

"It is not all right," said Mrs. Peters. "They did not ask your permission."

Jody didn't seem hurt. He was smiling. Everyone went up to him and asked him questions about his wheelchair. And about having to be in it.

"I wish I had a wheelchair," said Molly. "Handicapped kids get all the attention. Everyone wants to be their friend."

"My cousin gets to be in the Special Olympics," said Rachel.

"And they get to go to parties and picnics

and get on TV, and everybody helps them do everything," said Lisa.

"But some handicapped people can't walk," Kevin pointed out. "Some can't play ball and swim and stuff."

"My cousin can swim and play ball," said Rachel. "There are special teams for people with different abilities."

Molly thought about all the good things you got when you were handicapped. Jody even had a real job. But then she thought about having to be carried upstairs. She wouldn't like that. If she wanted to get upstairs in a hurry, or downstairs to Pee Wee Scouts, and there was no one to carry her, she'd have to wait!

"I'm glad I'm not in a wheelchair," whispered Mary Beth to Molly. "It wouldn't fit in my snow fort in winter."

"Yes, it would," said Jody, who had overheard Mary Beth. Mary Beth's face turned red. She hadn't meant for Jody to hear her.

62

"I build great big snow forts in winter, and I can get my chair in if I want to. But usually I don't use my wheelchair when I build snow forts."

Was there anything Jody couldn't do? thought Molly. Handicapped people must have a lot of extra pep, or take more vitamins. Maybe if you had a disability, you got something extra like a snow fort gene, or a job gene, or a guitar gene.

Mrs. Peters was holding up someone's leaf collection. "Has anyone else brought their hobby along to show us?" she asked.

Roger had brought another board with holes drilled in it.

Mary Beth brought her vase.

There were lots of stamp collections and salt and pepper shakers.

Rachel brought her skis.

And Jody brought some of his new compact discs.

Molly was not the only one whose hobby was new. Many of the Pee Wees had found new hobbies too.

Molly reached down into her book bag and took out her sweater. She raised her hand to show it.

"Yes, Molly," said Mrs. Peters.

"One of my fish died," she said. "And they didn't have any babies."

Some of the Pee Wees snickered. Fish having babies made them laugh.

"So I decided to knit," said Molly. "I am making my grandma and grandpa sweaters for Grandparents Day. And then I'm going to make some more to sell."

"Good for you," said Mrs. Peters. "Making a sweater must be very hard to do."

"It isn't," said Molly.

"Let's see, let's see!" shouted the Pee Wees.

Molly held up the sweater she had knitted. It did not look as good to her as she remembered.

"That's a *sweater*?" shouted Roger. "A sweater for an ant, maybe!"

"Or a squirrel." Sonny laughed.

All the Pee Wees were laughing now. Even

her best friend, Mary Beth, had a red face from trying not to laugh. Mary Beth, who was the one who had suggested this hobby!

Molly looked at the sweater in front of her.

One sleeve was long and skinny.

One was short and fat.

The back was tiny. There was no front.

And there were holes all over that Molly had not noticed before.

It looked so funny to her now that she burst out in laughter along with all the others.

Then she realized that this was her second hobby that had failed. And her laughter changed to tears. Was she going to be the only one without a hobby badge?

"I think you knit very well, Molly, for a beginner," said Mrs. Peters. "You just need more practice. And perhaps you should start with something easier than a sweater. Sweaters are not easy to knit."

Molly did not want to do something easy.

She wanted to do something hard. Hard and clever.

"I'd suggest a scarf," said Mrs. Peters. "A baby scarf."

That scarf again! Why in the world would Molly want to knit a baby scarf? Rat's knees! She began to wish she'd never heard the word *hobby*.

Molly stuffed the sweater back into her bag.

"It's all right," said Mary Beth kindly. "You can start over again. It just needs to be bigger. And more even," she added.

Molly wanted to throw the sweater into the rubbish. She didn't want to see it again.

"My mom is bringing my hobby," said Sonny. "I got a new hobby too. It was too big to carry."

All of a sudden there was a lot of racket on the stairs.

"Hey, what's that?" shouted Roger, looking up from drilling imaginary holes in Patty's arm with a soda straw. "It sounds like a dinosaur coming down here."

There was a dragging noise and a scraping

67

noise. There there was a bump, bump, bump noise.

"It's a burglar!" shouted Tim.

But it wasn't. It was Mrs. Stone bringing in Sonny's new hobby.

CHAPTER 7

The Extra-Clever Hobby at Last

Mrs. Stone came down the steps. In her arms was a big box. Behind her was another big box. Clump, clump, clump they came. Sonny's mother did not look happy. She looked tired. Her hair was falling in her face. Her sweater had orange powder all over it.

"It's my new hobby," boasted Sonny. He did not go to help his mother. Mrs. Peters pushed Roger and Kevin toward Mrs. Stone.

"Help her lift those onto the table," she said.

"Scouts are supposed to be helpers," whispered Molly. "Like in our song. And Sonny isn't even helping with his own hobby!"

69

Mrs. Stone brushed herself off and got a drink of water.

"What's in these things, Stone? Bricks?" yelled Roger.

"How did you know what my hobby is?" asked Sonny, pouting.

He opened one box. It was full of bricks.

"I collect them," said Sonny.

"Who'd collect *bricks*?" said Rachel.

"What can you do with them?" asked Patty.

"You can collect them, that's what," said Sonny.

"Sonny saw a brick in the alley by our house and decided he had to collect them," said his mother.

"All bricks look the same!" said Mary Beth.

"They do not!" shouted Sonny. "I've got red bricks here, and orange, and concrete bricks with holes in them. And here's a white one!"

"Big deal!" snorted Roger.

"It is a fine collection," said Mrs. Peters. "But a rather . . . heavy one."

"I like them," said Sonny, putting his arms around the boxes.

Molly rolled her eyes in disgust. At least now she knew what she *didn't* want to collect. And this proved that Sonny was not extra clever. There was no way his grandparents wanted a brick on their special day.

"I'm giving some of them to my grandpa at our program. He's building a barbecue in the backyard, and now he won't have to buy them," said Sonny proudly.

Maybe Sonny was more clever than Molly thought. And he surely was clever to get someone else to do all his work: to lug his hobby all the way to Scouts and down a flight of steps and up again.

"You'll have to wait for your father to come and get these," Mrs. Stone was saying. "I'm not lugging them all the way back up those steps."

"I want to take them with us," Sonny said, pouting.

"If Sonny gets a badge for picking up

bricks in the alley, I should get one for half a sweater," muttered Molly.

"Your sweater is better than bricks," said Mary Beth loyally.

But Mrs. Peters had sounded as if Molly should have another hobby, or else knit a baby scarf instead of a sweater. She would not knit a baby scarf. But what in the world would her new hobby be?

After everyone had looked at Sonny's bricks, Mrs. Peters asked if there were any other collections. She looked as if she hoped that there weren't.

Tim rattled a grocery bag. He raised his hand.

"I've got my collection in here," he said.

The Pee Wees gathered around Tim to look in his bag.

"Light bulbs!" said Rachel. "Glass light bulbs!"

"They're burned out!" said Tim proudly. "My dad just throws them away when they burn out, so I'm going to collect them."

"Hey, how many Scouts does it take to collect a light bulb, Noon?"

Before anyone could reply, Roger said, "One dumb one. Tim Noon."

Tim stuck his tongue out at Roger. Then Mrs. Peters took Roger aside and talked to him. Molly couldn't hear the words, but their leader was angry. She shook her finger at him. Then Roger sat down. His face was red, and he was quiet. Molly was glad he got in trouble. "It's about time," said Tracy.

"You could paint light bulbs," said Mary Beth. "You could paint faces on them and use them for Christmas tree ornaments."

"That is a very creative idea," said Mrs. Peters. "I'm glad to see you are thinking recycling!"

Rat's knees! Why didn't Molly think of that? Mrs. Peters loved to hear about things that could be used over and over again for something else.

The Scouts told their good deeds. (Roger's was helping Mrs. Stone carry the bricks. Talk about waiting till the last minute, thought

Molly.) Then they sang their song. All the way home, Molly wondered about her hobby.

"Why don't you just collect something easy, like matchboxes or postcards?" said Mary Beth.

"My dad won't let me have matches," said Molly. "And no one ever writes to me."

When Molly got home, she told her parents about her knitting.

"A new hobby will be my third hobby!" Molly complained.

"It seems like there's too much hullabaloo over a hobby," said Mr. Duff. "It shouldn't be this hard. When I was a boy, I played baseball in the empty lot and it was fun and it was a hobby, but I never worried about it."

"You weren't a Pee Wee Scout," said Molly. "And there aren't any empty lots around here. I couldn't hit a ball even if there were."

Mrs. Duff gave Molly a hug.

"Don't worry so much about it. You'll think of something good and natural soon."

But when? thought Molly. Grandparents Day and the program were coming fast.

That night, Molly tried and tried to think of a new hobby.

The next day she tried too.

The more she thought, the more confused she got.

"It seems like my hobby is trying to *find* a hobby!" she confided to Mary Beth after school one day.

"You should start a club for kids with no hobby!" Her friend laughed.

Molly was tired of thinking about it. She stopped at the store where she got her fish and looked in the window. She saw some greeting cards for Grandparents Day. I might as well get them a card, she said to herself.

Molly looked at all the cards. The ones with the good pictures on them did not have good verses. The ones with good verses had bad pictures.

"Rat's knees!" she said, stamping her foot. "I'll have to make one of my own."

Molly went home and sat down at her desk. She took a big piece of paper and cut it in half. She folded the halves. Then she drew

a picture of her grandma and grandpa sitting on their front porch. She drew a picture of herself with them. She colored it.

Inside she wrote, "Roses are red, violets are blue, Nobody's got a grandma and grandpa as nice as you."

She drew a rose in one corner. And a violet in another.

Then she cut and pasted an envelope to fit the card out of another piece of paper.

"Well, that's done," she said out loud. "But I still don't have a hobby."

Molly showed it to her parents. They said the same thing they did whenever she made them a card.

"Our Molly is very creative," said her father. "And a good poet."

"And an artist," said Mrs. Duff. "There's no card like the one you make yourself. Grandma and Grandpa will love it. They'll save it with all the other things you've made them."

When Molly showed Mary Beth her card,

Mary Beth said, "Will you make me one? I can send it with my vase."

Before long, the other Pee Wees wanted her to make them cards too!

"But make mine green," said Tim. "I like green."

"And make mine say something about farms," said Lisa. "My grandpa has a farm."

Molly drew Lisa on a pony.

She made Tim's card green.

And she drew a vase full of flowers on Mary Beth's.

"Well, Molly, I guess you found your hobby!" said Mrs. Peters at the next meeting.

"Really?" said Molly.

Was Mrs. Peters right? Could she have found her hobby after all this time and not even have known it?

Molly decided Mrs. Peters was right.

It was something she did well.

It was something she liked to do.

And it was something extra clever! Something she could do for Grandparents Day!

"It's my hobby!" said Molly to her friends.

"I can make valentines and Christmas cards and birthday cards! I can make wedding cards and baby cards and St. Patrick's Day cards!"

"You could make place cards for parties," said Rachel.

"Thank goodness you found a hobby at last, Duff," said Roger. "I was getting tired of hearing you moan about it."

After the meeting, Jody wheeled himself over to her.

"I like your card," he said. "I can't rhyme stuff like that."

"I could show you how," said Molly warmly. "It isn't hard. I've got this little book that tells which words rhyme."

"Really?" said Jody. "Can you come over to my house on Monday? My dad can get me colored paper and one of those books."

"You can use mine," said Molly. "Monday is fine."

Jody wrote down his address for Molly.

"Molly's got a boyfriend," sang Roger.

Molly blushed. She could feel her cheeks

turn as pink as the frosting on Mrs. Peters's cupcakes. She liked Jody just fine. But Kevin was the one she would marry.

The next day at recess time, Jody had invitations to pass out.

"My mom and dad said I could have a party," he said. "It's a week from Saturday. It's after Grandparents Day. It's just for kids."

All the Pee Wees got an invitation. So did some of Jody's other school friends.

"Bring your swimsuits, because we've got a hot tub," he said.

There was no end, it seemed to Molly, to Jody's surprises.

"I can't wait," said Mary Beth. "Let's go together," she said to Molly.

"My dad can drive us," said Rachel. "It might be after dark by the time we come home."

A nighttime party! It would be Molly's first.

But there was a lot to think about before that. Grandparents Day was almost upon them.

When Molly got home from school, she

82

thought about Mary Beth not having her grandparents there with the others. Even though she could share Molly's grandparents, it would be better to have someone special of her own.

When Molly mentioned this to her mother, she said, "What about that nice neighbor who helped you learn to knit? Wouldn't she be a good substitute grandma for Mary Beth? She is her neighbor and friend and knows the whole family. I'll bet she would be glad to come."

Molly ran to the phone. She looked up Mrs. Beal's phone number.

"Why, I'd love to come!" said Mrs. Beal when Molly invited her. "I'd love to be Mary Beth's grandma for the day."

When Molly hung up, she felt as if she'd done a good deed for Mary Beth and Mrs. Beal both.

"Good for you," said her dad when he came home from work and heard about it.

Molly decided to make Mrs. Beal a card too. She went to her room after dinner and folded a fresh white piece of paper. She drew a picture of a girl knitting. Inside she wrote

Roses are red
And violets are blue.
Mrs. Beal is a good knitter and teacher,
And a good grandmother too.
P.S. I love you. Molly.

On Sunday morning Mr. Duff went over to Mrs. Peters's house to help set up chairs and tables in the yard for the party.

Molly waited at home for her grandparents to arrive so they could go over together. Finally they did.

"We wouldn't have missed this for anything," said her grandma.

Just before they left for the party, the Duffs' phone rang.

"Guess what?" said Mary Beth to Molly. "My grandparents can come after all! They came up in time for the party!"

"But Mrs. Beal is going to be your grandmother today!" cried Molly. "I invited her!"

"Two grandmas isn't too many," said Mary Beth. "Lots of kids will have four grandparents there."

Molly hadn't thought of that. Some of the Pee Wees even had six grandparents!

"But I don't have another present for Mrs. Beal!" said Mary Beth.

"I wrote her a verse and made a card," said Molly. "I can make another one for you to give her."

Mary Beth thanked Molly, and they hung up. Molly ran upstairs to get a piece of paper. She would write the card on the way.

"Roses are red," she wrote in the car. "Violets are blue. I love my grandmas, Both number one and number two. Love and XXXX, Mary Beth Kelly."

She folded the card in half and felt good about being able to rhyme words so fast. This hobby was paying off more every day.

At the Peterses' house, everyone was getting out of cars. There were Pee Wees and little brothers and sisters and older brothers and sisters and parents and grandparents. Even some aunts and uncles came.

"The more the merrier," called Mrs. Peters. "We have enough food for an army."

All the parents brought food. Molly's mother made potato salad. Roger's father brought lots and lots of corn on the cob. There was lemonade and cold ham and cold chicken. There were cakes and cookies and pies. But the grandparents didn't have to bring anything. It was their special day.

Before there were any introductions, Mr. Peters lined the grandparents up for the first game.

"Each grandparent is wearing a baby picture of his or her grandson or grandaughter on their collar," he said. "Let's guess whose grandparents are whose by looking at the baby pictures."

The Pee Wees walked up and down the row of grandparents.

One baby was round and fat.

One had hair that stood up like a broom!

One looked mean and tough.

"That must be Roger," Mary Beth whispered to Molly.

Molly giggled.

The Pee Wees guessed and guessed. They all guessed wrong at first. Finally they guessed right. Kevin guessed the most right and got a prize: a big puzzle of the Grand Canyon to put together.

The mean baby wasn't Roger. It was Lisa!

The round fat baby was Rachel!

"I won lots of beauty contests when I was a baby," said Rachel.

"Ha," said Roger. "Try and win one now."

Rachel stuck out her tongue at Roger even though it was Grandparents Day. Molly didn't blame her.

After the game the grandparents opened presents.

Mrs. Beal hugged both Mary Beth and Molly tightly. "I am going to get these cards framed and hang them in my hall," she said. "I never saw anyone so talented who was only seven years old!"

"Molly is going to be a famous poet," said her grandfather proudly.

"She gets her talent from me," joked Mr. Duff.

"It was worth coming up here for such an exciting party," said Mary Beth's grandfather.

"I'm so glad I was invited," said Mrs. Beal.

"We are too," said Jody's grandma. "Jody has been so happy since he joined the Pee Wee Scouts. We are so glad we could meet so many of his new friends."

The next game was a game of croquet. Jody hit the balls from his wheelchair. In fact, he won the game!

"He's winning everything!" said Tim.

Tim was right. Jody won a water-balloon throw, and then a dart game.

Mrs. Beal won a ringtoss game, and Roger's grumpy-looking grandpa smiled when he got the most balls through a basketball hoop.

"My grandpa could be on a professional basketball team!" bragged Roger.

"I'll challenge him!" said Kevin's grandpa.

The two grandpas played and played till

they were all worn out. It was a tie. Each of them had gotten the ball through the hoop sixteen times.

When everyone was too tired for more games, the Pee Wees sang their Pee Wee Scout song. Then they all took plates and loaded them up with food.

Molly took a little bit of everything on the table. Even the olives and pickles. Some people sat in lawn chairs and ate. Some sat on the grass. But everyone got plenty to eat.

Roger had five desserts.

"Pig," said Rachel.

"Our family has big eaters in it," said Roger. "Because we all have big, developed muscles."

Roger flexed his arm for Rachel. She ignored him.

The fathers of the Pee Wee Scouts were beginning to pick up paper plates and napkins and litter. They were cleaning up before the badges were given out.

When the sun began to sink in the sky, Mr.

Peters turned the little lights on the trees on. They made a cozy glow come over the yard.

Mrs. Peters tapped a spoon on the table.

"And now after our nice day together, we will end it by giving out our hobby badges," she said.

Everyone sat up straight and tall to watch. Each Pee Wee listened for his or her name.

As Mrs. Peters called out each Scout's name, she announced the hobby and told what he or she had done or made. Then there was wild applause from the parents and grandparents and relatives of that Pee Wee Scout.

Mrs. Peters held up Mary Beth's vase. Her grandparents and Mrs. Beal clapped and clapped. "It's beautiful!" they cried.

Then she held up Sonny's bricks. Molly wondered when she would call her name.

Tim's light bulbs were next.

And then at last, Mrs. Peters called, "Molly Duff!"

When Molly walked up to the table to get her badge, Mrs. Peters said, "It took Molly a

little while to find her hobby, but it was worth waiting for."

Everyone clapped as Molly pinned her badge onto her blouse.

Roger whistled through his teeth.

"Hey, I know why you chose that hobby," he said as she went to sit back down. "You chose it so you could make cards for us guys and use it for a good deed!"

Molly was too happy to pay any attention to Roger.

Everything had turned out so well!

She had a hobby at last.

It was extra clever because she had used it at Grandparents Day for a gift.

She had her brand-new hobby badge.

Her grandparents and Mrs. Beal had come to the party and had a good time.

And on top of that, she had a new friend! She was going to Jody's house on Monday. And to his party on Saturday. A party that might not be over until after dark!

Rat's knees! Sometimes being a Pee Wee Scout was the most fun thing in the world!

Pee Wee Scout Song
(to the tune of "Old MacDonald Had a Farm")

Scouts are helpers, Scouts have fun,
Pee Wee, Pee Wee Scouts!
We sing and play when work is done,
Pee Wee, Pee Wee Scouts!

With a good deed here,
And an errand there,
Here a hand, there a hand,
Everywhere a good hand.

Scouts are helpers, Scouts have fun,
Pee Wee, Pee Wee Scouts!

Pee Wee Scout Pledge

We love our country
And our home,
Our school and neighbors too.

As Pee Wee Scouts
We pledge our best
In everything we do.